The Bee's Secret

Written by **Marilyn Grohoske Evans**

Illustrated by **Jim Madsen**

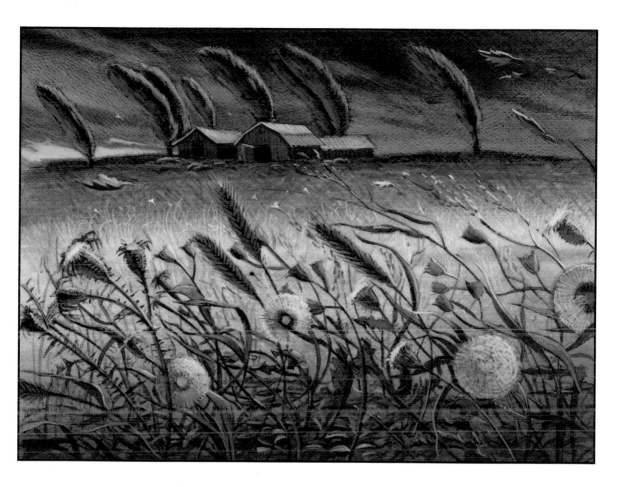

Rain pounds the earth.

Winds whip the trees and flowers.

At last the storm ends.

A moan comes from the beehive.

The humming grows louder.

The bees are hungry!

The cleaner bees can't clean.

The nurse bees can't nurse.

The wax-maker bees can't make wax.

The fanner bees can't fan.

The guard bees can't guard.

And the queen can't lay eggs to make new baby bees.

The hive is out of honey!

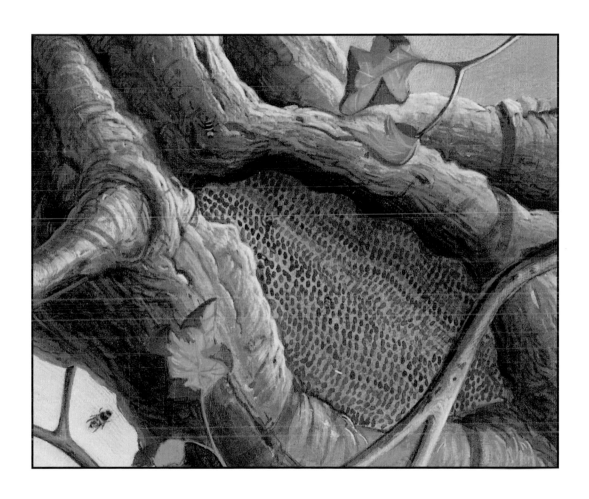

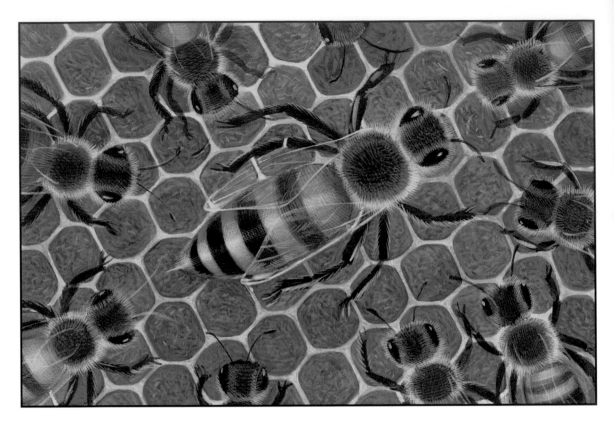

"Hurry! Hurry!" hums the queen.

"Go out and find nectar and pollen!"

The queen's daughters

zoom from the hive,

but they return quickly.

The rains and winds

have crushed the flowers

that give the bees

their nectar and pollen.

One fuzzy bee, the smallest bee of all,

flies in front of the queen.

She hums loudly,

but the other bees ignore her.

Still humming,

she flies out of the hive.

She flies to the north.

Then she flies to the south.

She is growing tired.

As she flies over the farmer's pond,

a sweet, new smell

rises from the wet grass.

She circles back and flies lower.

There, beside the barn, almost hidden,

is a small patch of pink flowers!

The little bee lands gently

on one velvet petal.

Her pointed tongue

and straw-like mouth

suck up the flower's sweet juices.

As she drinks,

grains of dusty, yellow pollen

cling to her legs and body.

She darts on to the next flower,

and the next, until at last she is full.

Now she must hurry home

and tell her sisters

about her secret nectar spot.

She looks at the sun.

It will help her remember this place

and find her way home.

At the hive,

her sisters rush to meet her.

But she buzzes away

and begins to dance.

Her body wags and quivers

in the secret dance

of the bee family.

The lazy "8" she has drawn

in her dance

tells her sisters exactly

where the sweet flowers grow.

She stops just long enough

for them to smell and taste

the rich nectar.

Again she dances.

Suddenly her sisters dance

around her.

They have read her dance.

Humming loudly,

they zoom from the hive.

As the smallest bee rests,

the other bees go to work.

Once again, the queen's beehive

is alive and buzzing.